ER
FLA 8/01

Play Day

The Sound of Long A

By Alice K. Flanagan

The Child's World®, Inc.

Today is play day.

Kay plays house
with Fay.

Ray plays with clay.

Kate plays on skates.

James plays with games.

Shane plays with a toy train.

Tracy plays with her bird Casey.

Brady plays with his
dog Lady.

Jamie plays with her
pig Amy.

Can you name more boys and girls at play?

Word List

Amy	James	plays
Brady	Jamie	Ray
Casey	Kate	Shane
clay	Kay	skates
day	Lady	today
Fay	name	Tracy
games	play	train

Note to Parents and Educators

The books in the Phonics series of the Wonder Books are based on current research which supports the idea that our brains are pattern detectors rather than rules appliers. This means children learn to read easier when they are taught the familiar spelling patterns found in English. As children encounter more complex words, they have greater success in figuring out these words by using the spelling patterns.

Throughout the 35 books, the texts provide the reader with the opportunity to practice and apply knowledge of the sounds in natural language. The 10 books on the long and short vowels introduce the sounds using familiar onsets and rimes, or spelling patterns, for reinforcement. For example, the word "cat" might be used to present the short "a" sound, with the letter "c" being the onset and "-at" being the rime. This approach provides practice and reinforcement of the short "a" sound, as there are many familiar words made with the "-at" rime.

The 21 consonants and the 4 blends ("ch," "sh," "th," and "wh") use many of these same rimes. The letter(s) before the vowel in a word are considered the onset. Changing the onset allows the consonant books in the series to maintain the practice and reinforcement of the rimes. The repeated use of a word or phrase reinforces the target sound.

The number on the spine of each book facilitates arranging the books in the order that children acquire each sound. The books can also be arranged into groups of long vowels, short vowels, consonants, and blends. All the books in each grouping have their numbers printed in the same color on the spine. The books can be grouped and regrouped easily and quickly, depending on the teacher's needs.

The stories and accompanying photographs in this series are based on time-honored concepts in children's literature: Well-written, engaging texts and colorful, high-quality photographs combine to produce books that children want to read again and again.

Dr. Peg Ballard
Minnesota State University, Mankato

Photo Credits

All photos © copyright: Photo Edit: 5, 6 (David Young-Wolff), 13 (Robert Brenner),
14, 17 (Myrleen Ferguson), 21 (Paul Conkle); Tony Stone Images: 2 (Bob Thomas),
9 (Gary Holscher), 10 (Peter Cade); Unicorn: 18 (Joel Dexter). Cover: Photo Edit/
Laura Dwight.

Photo Research: Alice Flanagan
Design and production: Herman Adler Design Group

Library of Congress Cataloging-in-Publication Data

Flanagan, Alice K.
    Play day : the sound of "long a" / by Alice K. Flanagan
    p. cm. — (Wonder books)
    Summary : Simple text about playing and repetition of the letter
"a" help readers learn how to use the "long a" sound.
    ISBN 1-56766-730-9 (lib. bdg. : alk. paper)
    [1. Play Fiction. 2. Alphabet.] I. Title. II. Series: Wonder books
(Chanhassen, Minn.)
PZ7.F59824Pl   1999
[E]—dc21   99-31939
                                                    CIP